Anytime
Stories
COLLECTION

A
MOUSE WORKS
STORYBOOK COLLECTION

Written by Rita Balducci, Jamie Simons, and Sheryl Kahn
Penciled by Orlando de la Paz and Ed Murrieta
Painted by John and Phillip Hom and the Alvin White Studio

Printed and bound in the United States of America
10 9 8 7 6 5 4 3 2 1

Table of Contents

The Friendship Bridge

The bridge crossing the shallow stream in the Hundred-Acre Wood had just been painted. Very important-looking signs that said WET PAINT! KEEP OFF! stood guard at both ends. But whoever had painted the bridge had left poor Eeyore stuck on one side, and the rest of his friends on the other!

"Don't worry, Eeyore!" Pooh called. "The paint should be dry soon!" But each time Pooh tapped the bridge with his hand, it came back smudged with fresh paint.

Eeyore sighed. Things like this were always happening to him.

Sadly, the friends gazed across the water at each other. It seemed that the paint was taking a very long time to dry.

Eeyore hung his head and looked at his reflection in the water. "Just my luck," was all he could say.

Suddenly a loud, familiar noise caught everyone's attention.

WET PAINT! KEEP OFF!

BOUNCE! BOUNCE! BOUNCE!

"Halloooo!" bellowed Tigger. "Hoo-hoo-hoo! Whatcha doin'?"

"W-w-well, we wanted to play with Eeyore over there, but the bridge…" Piglet didn't even get to finish his sentence before Tigger had bounced onto the wet bridge.

"Yuck!" cried Tigger, bouncing back to shore and shaking the paint from his feet. "Tiggers hate wet paint."

Then Tigger sat up proudly. "I will get to Eeyore," he said. "Watch me bounce right over the water."

Pooh and Piglet started to protest, but Tigger wouldn't listen. He took a running start and **BOUNCE!** He landed right in the middle of the stream.

"Yeow!" he said, shaking himself off and showering Pooh and Piglet in the process.

It took a lot to discourage Tigger. He tried again and again. Each time he landed in the water, he shook himself off all over Pooh and Piglet.

WET PAINT!
KEEP OFF!

Piglet wiped the water off his face and Pooh wrung out his shirt. "Since we're all wet," said Piglet, "why don't we just wade across to Eeyore?"

What an excellent idea! Pooh and Piglet held hands and slowly waded across the shallow stream to Eeyore.

"And I didn't even have to get wet!" Eeyore said happily as the friends climbed up the bank to meet him. At that moment, Tigger bounced up to join them, spraying water all over Eeyore, after all.

"It figures," Eeyore said, standing in a puddle.

Soon Rabbit came by. He glanced at the wet group and then tapped the bridge with a finger. "Ah, nice and dry," he said, pulling off the WET PAINT sign. Then he marched across the bridge and pulled off the other sign.

"Well," said Eeyore as they watched Rabbit disappear into the Hundred-Acre Wood, "now that the bridge is dry and we're all wet, does anyone want to go swimming?"

A Honey of a Cake

One chilly autumn morning, Rabbit decided he'd make a delicious honey cake. "I'll bake the best cake ever," he told Pooh, Piglet, and Tigger. The trio could just picture the delicious dessert—sticky-sweet and hot, right out of the oven.

"Let us help you, Rabbit," Pooh pleaded, hoping he'd get to lick a spoon or two.

"No, no, no," Rabbit insisted, lining up his mixing bowls on the kitchen table. "I want this cake to be the best—and too many cooks spoil the honey cake."

"Aw, come on, Long Ears," Tigger urged. "We won't spoil your cake."

"We'll listen to all your directions," Piglet said. "We promise."

Finally Rabbit gave in. "All right," he said.

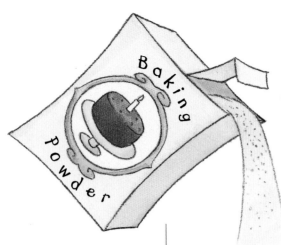

"But do exactly as I say—and only when I tell you to."

He showed Piglet how to crack the eggs neatly, without getting any shells into the bowl. Tigger buttered the pan with his tail—so the cake wouldn't stick—and Pooh beat the batter until it was smooth.

"Let's see," Rabbit said, thumbing through his cookbook. "What am I forgetting? Oh, yes! Baking powder! That's what makes the cake grow big, you know." He carefully measured and mixed in the baking powder.

Pooh, Piglet, and Tigger thought to themselves: *A big honey cake would be wonderful, but an even **BIGGER** one would be even better.*

Pooh waited until Rabbit was bending over the oven and then added more baking powder to the cake. While Rabbit carefully stacked his bowls in the sink, Piglet added more. And while Rabbit was returning his cookbook to the shelf, Tigger added even more.

"It's ready to bake," said Rabbit, as he closed the oven door.

The three friends couldn't wait for Rabbit to see how much better—and **BIGGER**—the cake would be with their help. They waited patiently for Rabbit to check the oven.

"Oh, my! Oh, my!" they heard him call from the kitchen, and they raced in to see the look of happy surprise on Rabbit's face.

Rabbit looked surprised, but not very happy. The cake was **ENORMOUS,** and it was growing bigger every minute. It stretched from wall to wall and from floor to ceiling. Everything in Rabbit's kitchen was surrounded by cake.

"What have you done?" Rabbit cried, trying to keep his dishes from being knocked off their shelves. "Look at my kitchen! There's cake everywhere!"

"Can we help?" Piglet asked.

"No!" shouted Rabbit. "Haven't you done enough?"

"But I've got a Tigger-ific idea to clean up this cake," said Tigger, winking at his friends.

Two hours later, the only piece of cake left was just the size of the baking pan—and there were no rumblies in the tummies of Pooh, Tigger, Piglet, or Rabbit.

"Dee-licious!" said Pooh, smacking his lips. They all agreed— even Rabbit—that it had been one honey of a cake, indeed!

The Best Gift of All

Little Roo drew a big red circle on the calendar, reminding him that a very special date was just a week away.

"It's almost Mother's Day, Pooh," he told his friend. "And I have to give my mother the best gift of all."

"Might I suggest a nice, big pot of honey?" Pooh asked, rubbing his tummy.

Roo thought hard. "I don't know," he said. "We have lots of honey pots."

"One can never have too much honey," Pooh interrupted, helping himself to a sticky-sweet smackerel.

"Thanks, Pooh—but I think I'll ask our friends what they think," Roo said. He hopped off to find Tigger, Owl, Rabbit, and Eeyore.

"Oh, Owl!" Roo shouted up to the top of his wise friend's tree house.

"I say, who's there?" Owl asked. He closed the book he was reading and went to the door. "Oh, it's you," he said, looking down at Roo.

"What's the best gift of all?" Roo called.

"A good book," Owl stated. "That's the best gift for me."

"Oh," sighed Roo. "Mama already has lots of books she reads to me." Roo hopped off to see Rabbit, who was busy watering his garden.

"Careful!" he called as the little kangaroo bounced between his rows of perfectly planted carrots and cabbage. "Stop jumping about there! A garden is a very serious place."

"Hmm," Roo thought as he watched Rabbit rake lines in the brown soil. "Do you think my mother would like to start a garden? I want to give her the best gift of all for Mother's Day."

"A rake is a very practical gift," Rabbit said, waving his high in the air. "I'd certainly want one."

"A rake? Don't be ridickerlous!" said a voice from behind a patch of tall sunflowers. Suddenly Tigger bounced out, pouncing on Rabbit and knocking him to the ground.

"You want to know the best gift of all, kiddo?" he asked Roo. "A pogo stick, so you can bounce as high as me!"

"Oh," said Roo. "But Mama got *me* a pogo stick for a present." Roo hopped away, looking for another suggestion.

Soon he found Eeyore relaxing under a shady tree. "What do you think is the best gift of all, Eeyore?" Roo asked.

"I don't know," Eeyore answered. "But I'd like a day of just doing nothing."

Mother's Day came, and Roo was still uncertain. "No one can tell me for sure what is the best gift of all," he sighed.

Pooh put his arm around his little friend. "Don't worry, Roo," he said. "Your mother will love any gift as long as it's from your heart."

"That's it!" cried Roo, and he raced home to give his mother the present. He hopped into Kanga's arms, gave her a big hug, and covered her face with kisses.

"Oh, Roo," Kanga said, cuddling her son. "What a wonderful Mother's Day present."

"Pooh was right," Roo said, snuggling in his mother's pocket. "Love is the best gift of all."

Rabbit's Reunion

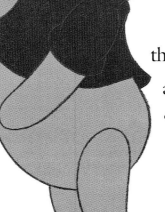

Rabbit was always a very busy person, but today was the busiest Pooh had ever seen him. As Pooh stood in the door of Rabbit's kitchen, Rabbit bustled around him, a dust mop in one hand and a sponge in the other, cleaning, cleaning, cleaning.

"Oh, Pooh!" said a startled Rabbit. "What are you doing here?"

"I was wondering if you might happen to have a smidgen of honey somewhere about the house?" Pooh asked politely. "You see, I'm a bit rumbly in…"

"…in your tumbly," Rabbit finished. "In the pantry, Pooh, look in the pantry."

Rabbit certainly was very distracted. And when Pooh saw the ten honey jars stacked neatly on Rabbit's pantry shelf, he knew that Rabbit must be having company.

One look at Rabbit's calendar told Pooh that he was right, for there was a big circle around tomorrow's date, and the words "Rabbit's Family Reunion" printed next to it.

"A family reunion!" Pooh thought excitedly.

Pooh thanked Rabbit and hurried home.
"I would very much like to meet some of Rabbit's family," he thought. And right there and then, Pooh had a very good idea. "I will pretend that I am one of Rabbit's relations," he decided. "Then I can meet them all for myself!"

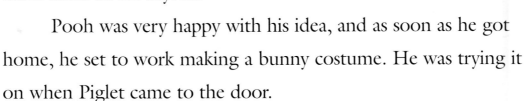

Pooh was very happy with his idea, and as soon as he got home, he set to work making a bunny costume. He was trying it on when Piglet came to the door.

"Hello, Pooh?" called Piglet. "What are you doing?"

Pooh quickly explained his plan to Piglet, who cried, "Ooh! I love costume parties! Do you think Rabbit would mind if I came, too?" And with that he hurried off to start his own bunny outfit.

It was a strange parade of rabbits that marched through the Hundred-Acre Wood the following morning. Piglet had met Tigger and Eeyore on his way home, and they all wanted to meet Rabbit's many relations.

So there they were—ears, fuzzy tails, and whiskers—all doing their best to be bunnies.

But it was a very unhappy Rabbit who opened the front door. In his hand he held a letter. "It's from my cousins," Rabbit said sadly. "There are new baby bunnies in the family, and so they won't be coming."

Rabbit's shoulders sagged as he folded the letter. All that work for nothing! Then he noticed his friends' strange costumes.

"Well, well, well!" he said, starting to smile. "It looks like there's going to be a rabbit party today, after all!"

And, as Rabbit ushered his friends inside, he realized that a family of good friends was a wonderful thing to have!

Help for Hiccups

One morning Tigger awoke feeling funny. His toes tingled and his nose wriggled, and he bounced out of bed with a loud **HICCUP!**

"I'll just hold my breath," he said, bouncing higher and higher with every **HICCUP!** "Or sip some water." But no matter what he did, his hiccups wouldn't stop.

"I better get some **HICCUP!** help," he said, and he bounced right out his door and down the path into Rabbit's garden. "I have a **HICCUP!** problem," he called, bouncing all over Rabbit's beautiful vegetables.

"You're trampling my carrots! You're squishing my squash!" Rabbit cried.

"Can't **HICCUP!** help it!" replied Tigger.

"Have you tried wiggling your ears and winking one eye?" asked Rabbit.

Tigger tried, but it didn't work. So he bounced off to find another remedy.

"Hiya, **HICCUP!** Owl," Tigger said, bouncing into his wise friend's home. "You're smart—you must know a cure for the **HICCUP!**"

"You must recite the alphabet backwards, then forwards," Owl advised.

So Tigger tried it: "Z, Y, X, **HICCUP!** A, B, C." He bounced right into Owl's bookshelf, knocking all of his books to the floor. "Sorry, Owl!" he **HICCUP**ed as he hurried off to find Pooh.

"I have a cure that always works," Pooh said, demonstrating. "You stand on one foot while you rub your tummy with one hand and eat some delicious honey with the other."

"HICCUP! HICCUP! HICCUP! It seems to make it worse!" Tigger said. His bouncing was out of control. All of Pooh's honey pots tumbled off the cupboard shelves and onto the floor.

"This is quite serious," said Owl as he and Rabbit looked in on the mess Tigger was making in Pooh's house. "We must find a way to cure Tigger."

"Think hard," instructed Owl. "How did this start?"

"I was sleeping and I felt a feather from my pillow tickle my nose," answered Tigger. "The next thing I knew—**HICCUP!**"

"Hmmm," Owl said. "That gives me an idea." He huddled with Rabbit and Pooh. "I think we can make Tigger's hiccups stop the same way they started," he said. Rabbit and Pooh nodded—they knew what needed to be done.

"Hey! **HICCUP!** What's going on?" Tigger asked, as Owl, Rabbit, and Pooh surrounded him. They tickled his tummy until he wriggled and giggled.

"Stop! Stop!" Tigger laughed. "That tickles!" By the time they stopped tickling Tigger, something else had stopped, too. "My hiccups—they're gone! I'm cured!"

"Hooray!" cheered his friends.

"HICCUP!"

The friends stared at Tigger.

"Just kidding," he chuckled. Then he bounced happily back home.

Pooh's Bright Idea

It was a warm summer evening, and Pooh and Piglet were watching fireflies light up the Hundred-Acre Wood.

Suddenly Pooh sat up and stared at the honey tree. "Why, of course..." whispered Pooh.

"Did you just have an idea, Pooh?" Piglet asked.

Pooh nodded. "Piglet," he whispered, "do you see those fireflies over by the honey tree? Why, if I were one of them, I could ever so quietly visit the honeybees. They would never mind me a bit. In fact, they would never even notice me. And if I happened to get a little hungry, wouldn't they let a harmless firefly have a smackerel of honey?"

Before Piglet could say a word, Pooh hurried into his house. He returned carrying a very large flashlight and some string.

"You tie the light around my tummy with this string," Pooh said excitedly, handing over the flashlight, "and I shall hum and flutter like a firefly. The bees will never suspect a thing."

Piglet did as Pooh asked, and off Pooh went to climb the honey tree.

But before Pooh was very far up the tree, the flashlight began to slip. It slid around his back and almost off. Pooh held onto the tree while the swinging light flopped over and shone right into Kanga's house.

"Oh, dear! Oh, dear!" cried Kanga, running outside. "Was that a lightning flash? I must close all the windows before it starts to rain!"

Piglet shook his head and pointed to Pooh. Kanga and Roo watched Pooh waving the flashlight wildly as he tried to tie it back in place.

The light woke Owl next. He stepped outside, blinking his eyes and clearing his throat.

"I say!" he said. "I do say! Can it be morning already?" Then he peered into the darkness until his eyes focused on Pooh. "What's going on?" asked Owl.

"Watch and see!" called Pooh to his sleepy friend.

At last Pooh reached the hive. "I'm going in!" he whispered loudly to Piglet, Owl, Kanga, and Roo, who had gathered below. But the flashlight bumped against a knobby tree branch and shone directly into the hive itself, waking up the hundreds of sleeping bees.

The bees were not fooled for a minute, not even when Pooh hummed and flashed the flashlight on and off. They were grouchy and tired as they swarmed out of the hive after Pooh, chasing him to the ground. Pooh climbed down the tree as fast as he could.

"Oh, don't be disappointed, Pooh," said Piglet, taking Pooh's hand. "It seemed like a good idea."

Just then Roo hopped outside, carrying a huge jar of honey under one arm. "Mama," he called to Kanga. "How about this jar? Can I use it to catch the fireflies?"

Kanga laughed. "Why, Roo dear! That jar is full of honey!"

Pooh stepped up with a very good suggestion. "If I help you empty your jar, Roo," he began, "then you can fill it with fireflies."

Peace and quiet settled once more on the Hundred-Acre Wood as Pooh licked the last of Roo's honey from his hands. The empty honey jar flickered in the darkness with all the fireflies Roo had caught.

"Time for bed, Roo!" Kanga called. Pooh helped Roo open the jar, and the friends watched the fireflies scatter into the night.

"Thanks," Pooh called to them softly. "I knew we'd make a honey of a team!"

Piglet and the Boowuzzle Monster

I t was a dark and stormy night," read Owl, as Pooh, Tigger, Rabbit, and Piglet gathered around him to hear a spooky ghost story.

"Just like th-th-th-this one?" Piglet asked, covering his ears as thunder crashed outside Owl's tree house.

"It's just a story, Piglet," Pooh assured him.

"Yeah, it's not real," Tigger chimed in.

"May I continue?" Owl asked, tapping his wing on the arm of his rocking chair.

"Yes, please do," sniffed Rabbit.

"In the shadows, the boowuzzle monster's one eye glowed yellow—"

"Oh, no!" Piglet ducked under a chair. Thunder crashed again. Piglet scooted under the rug.

"He made his way up the tree house ladder, till he reached the door," Owl continued. "Then with one swipe of his powerful claw, he knocked it down!"

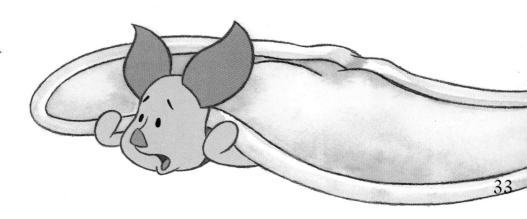

"What happened then, Owl?" Pooh asked.

"I d-d-don't want to know," Piglet said, shaking and quaking.

"You're not scared, are ya?" Tigger said. He peeked beneath the rug and shouted "Boo!"

Piglet jumped and ran to hide behind Owl's chair.

"I'm not scared," Piglet said, trying to hold his chin up.

"Of course you're scared," said Rabbit. "You're scared of your own shadow, Piglet!"

"Am not!" Piglet protested.

The argument was interrupted by a loud pounding on Owl's door. The five friends looked at each other.

"You don't suppose…" Pooh gulped.

"Nah," said Tigger. "That stuff only happens in stories."

Suddenly the door flew open and a shadowy figure appeared in the doorway. It stared at them with an evil, glowing, yellow eye.

"Run for your lives!" screamed Rabbit. "It's the boowuzzle monster!"

"Help! Help!" yelled Tigger.

"Oh, my! Oh, my!" called Owl.

"We're doomed!" said Pooh, pulling his red shirt up over his head.

Piglet was frozen with fear, but he had to save his friends. He spotted a broom in the corner and quickly grabbed it, pointing it at the mean monster.

"T-t-t-take that!" he shouted.

The boowuzzle backed away. "Hey, Piglet, cut it out!" it said.

That's funny, thought Piglet. The monster sounded familiar.

Piglet put down the broom and let the boowuzzle step into the light of Owl's house. It was Christopher Robin!

"I just came to see if you were okay in the storm," he said, turning off the yellow beam of his flashlight.

"We thought you were the boowuzzle monster," Pooh said.

"Silly old bear!" said Christopher Robin.

"And Piglet was the one who saved us," said Tigger. "Good going, pal!"

"You were very brave, indeed," said Owl.

"Yes, you did come to our aid," admitted Rabbit.

"It was nothing," blushed Piglet.

But he couldn't help beaming with pride when his friends shouted, "Hip-hip hooray for our hero, Piglet!"

35

Pooh and the Pot of Gold

There was a time in the Hundred-Acre Wood when the rain came and would not go away. Polite company knows that short stays are best, but the rain had never learned this lesson. Day after day it stayed on, till everyone was cross. Even Pooh lost his hummy ways. He'd been trapped inside for days with only his cupboard of honey for a friend. And every day it rained, the cupboard got a little more bare.

Finally Pooh decided to talk to the rain. "It's been ever so nice having you stay, but while you are here the sun won't visit, and we miss his company, too."

Perhaps the rain took pity on Pooh. Or maybe the rain missed home. Whichever way it was, the rain gathered up his drops, leaving the sun room to shine. And as the sun and rain touched coming in and going out, their hug left behind a rainbow.

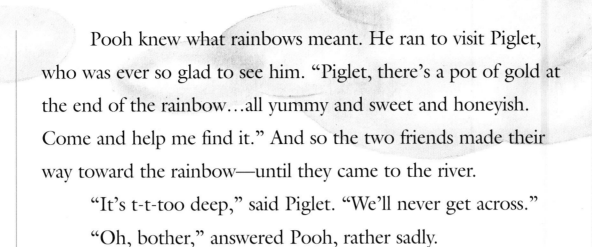

Pooh knew what rainbows meant. He ran to visit Piglet, who was ever so glad to see him. "Piglet, there's a pot of gold at the end of the rainbow…all yummy and sweet and honeyish. Come and help me find it." And so the two friends made their way toward the rainbow—until they came to the river.

"It's t-t-too deep," said Piglet. "We'll never get across."

"Oh, bother," answered Pooh, rather sadly.

"Hello-o-o," called a voice from the other side of the river. Pooh looked up to see whose voice it could be.

"Tigger!" cried Pooh. "How did you get there?"

"I bounced," said Tigger, as he bounced across to Pooh.

"Could you bounce us across?" asked Pooh.

"Hold on!" yelled Tigger, and he did just that. "But where are you going?"

"T-t-to the pot of honey at the end of the rainbow," offered Piglet.

"Adventure!" cried Tigger. "Can I come, too?"

And so the three friends made their way toward the rainbow, until they came to the soggy bogs. Pooh would have sat down to think, but Owl happened by.

"What are the three of you doing?" he asked.

"Looking for the pot of honey at the end of the rainbow," Tigger told him.

"You mean gold," said Owl.

"That's right," said Tigger. "A pot filled with runny, honey gold."

"C-c-could you take us there?" asked Piglet.

"I could lead you there," Owl said. He sailed into the air and called to the friends below, "Follow me!" Pooh, Tigger, and Piglet hurried after Owl. Soon they reached the rainbow's end, but there was no pot of any kind to be found.

"There may not be gold at the end of the rainbow," said Piglet brightly, "but I see a treasure right where we're standing."

Being a bear of very little brain, at first Pooh was befuddled. But as he looked over at his friends standing in the golden sunlight, he understood what Piglet meant. Pooh agreed with all his heart that their friendship was as precious as any pot of gold, and as sweet as a hundred honey pots.

Eeyore's Amazing Adventure

Tah-dum, dee-day, today is perfect in every way," Pooh sang as he and Christopher Robin strolled through the Hundred-Acre Wood. The sun was shining, the birds were singing, and Pooh was carrying a big new pot of honey back to his home.

"Perfect for an explore, you mean," said Christopher Robin as they saw Eeyore. "Nice day, Eeyore!" he called to his friend.

"Just like yesterday," Eeyore replied, "and the day before, and the day before that. Just plain humdrum."

"Humdrum?" Christopher Robin asked. "Surely you must be mistaken, Eeyore. Today is anything but humdrum. There's an adventure right under your nose, if you look for it."

Eeyore looked down at his nose.

"Looks like a nose to me," he said.

"I don't see any adventure."

"Perhaps we could look somewhere else," Pooh said, pointing to the woods.

"Let's snoop around," Christopher Robin said. "That's what famous explorers on safari do." They tiptoed through the tall grass and bushes, careful not to disturb the wild beasts that might be there. Eeyore was only a few steps ahead when he heard Pooh cry out for help.

"Eeyore!" he shouted. "Help!

"Pooh's stuck in quicksand!" Christopher Robin cried.

Eeyore found a long vine and dragged it over to Pooh. "Hold on, I'll get you out," he said, tugging the vine in his mouth with all his might. "Almost there," Eeyore said, pulling the vine tight around a tree trunk. Pooh would be free in no time.

Suddenly a loud roar came from behind the tree.

"Run, Eeyore! Forget about us!" cried Pooh.

"It's a ferocious tiger!"

42

The tiger tackled Eeyore, throwing him and the vine to the ground. Eeyore closed his eyes. He could hear the tiger growling in his floppy ears.

"Whatcha up to?" it said. Eeyore opened his eyes and found himself nose to nose with Tigger—not a tiger at all. Eeyore blinked and looked around, too surprised to answer Tigger's question.

Pooh was sitting in a puddle of sticky honey—not quicksand—and Christopher Robin's jump rope, not a vine, lay on the ground beside him.

"This wasn't such a humdrum day, after all," Pooh said, licking the honey from his hands.

"See, Eeyore? You can always have an amazing adventure with a little imagination," said Christopher Robin.

But Eeyore wasn't listening—he was too busy imagining what tomorrow, and the day after, and the day after that might bring.

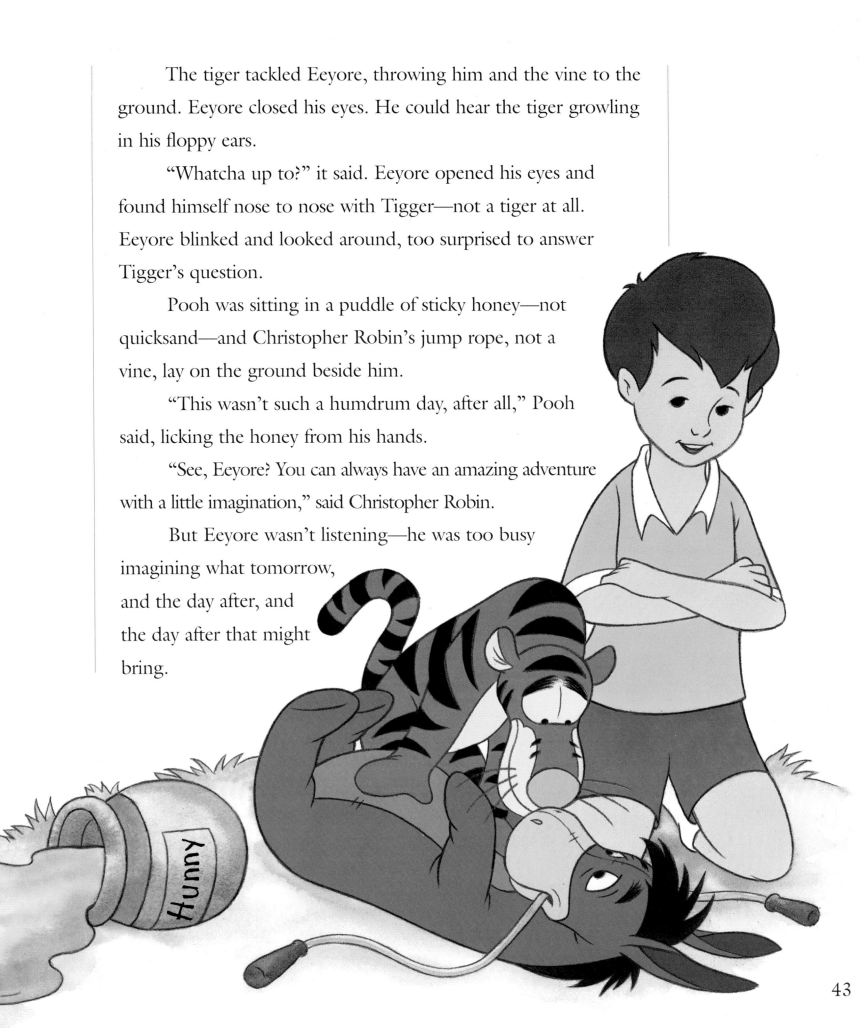

43

Pooh's Garden

Pooh awoke one spring morning to discover that his yard was not a yard at all. It was more like a very boggy mess. The snow had melted, leaving puddles of mud—good for sloppy splashing, but not much good for lolling, which is what Pooh had in mind.

Pooh would have said, "Oh, bother," but he didn't get the chance. For just as the words formed in his mind, Rabbit knocked on his door.

"Why, Pooh," said Rabbit, "you are looking a bit grumbly for a bear. Is there anything I can help you with?"

Pooh showed Rabbit his very boggy mess, but Rabbit didn't see it that way. "A garden!" he cried. And with that Rabbit ran off to get his gardening tools.

"A garden," said Pooh. "One great tree with bees right outside my door and a grassy patch for eating honey and lolling round." The idea turned Pooh scrum-diddley with delight.

Rabbit returned with one wheelbarrow, two hoes, three rakes, four shovels, and five packets of carrot seeds, which he planted in six rows. "That's very nice," said Pooh to Rabbit. "On certain days I could eat carrots. But I was thinking of something maybe a little more golden."

"Golden?" asked Tigger, as he bounced into Pooh's garden. "Look what I've got! Rabbit told me you were planting, so I brought corn."

"Do you think corn attracts bees?" asked Pooh weakly.

"No, but tomato plants do," said Piglet, as he showed up with several. "At least, I think maybe they do."

Tomato honey? thought Pooh. Not wanting to hurt Piglet's feelings, he only said, "Thank you."

"Hope you don't mind one more helper," Eeyore said, dropping a bunch of thistles. "No one invited me, but I thought your garden could use some crunch. I can take them away if you want."

"Oh, no," said Pooh. "Please stay. I'll even help you plant the thistles. They'd be my favorite if I'd ever had any." Then to himself he said rather softly, "Which I haven't, because what pooh bears like is honey."

All day long more of Pooh's friends came by to help plant his garden.

But no one had thought to bring a tree with bees.

Pooh tried to hint. As he worked, he hummed out loud, "What Pooh likes best is gold and runny, and smells an awful lot like honey!" But no one paid him any mind.

By the end of the day there were six rows of carrots, seven rows of corn, eight tomato plants, nine thistle patches, ten rows of peppers, and eleven rows of cauliflower, but no trees with bees.

Well, thought Pooh as he looked at his garden, *there's no honey tree and no grassy spot, but there is an awful lot of everything else.*

Rabbit said, "See? A garden is just the thing."

Pooh looked out on his very large garden, which would take a very large amount of work, and felt rather weak. But since his friends had been so generous, he politely said, "Thank you. When everything is ready to be picked, you must all come back for a party. There will be carrots for Rabbit, corn for Tigger, tomatoes for Piglet, thistles for Eeyore, peppers for Roo, and cauliflower for Kanga."

"And," said Rabbit, pulling out a honey pot he'd been hiding, "honey for Pooh."

Roo and the Baby-Sitter

Kanga was a wonderful mother, always doing very motherly things. She counted up Roo's shirts, and folded them neatly, and looked for spots from time to time. Since she was such a good mother, when Kanga went out, she looked for someone to baby-sit Roo, someone who would do good motherly things, too.

Thinking Eeyore might do, Kanga asked him, "Are you patient?"

"Very patient," replied Eeyore.

"Are you caring?"

"I care deeply, but no one notices," answered Eeyore.

"Then you are just the one I am looking for. Eeyore, would you be so kind as to watch Roo?"

"You want me to come to your house? Well, no one's ever...but maybe they shouldn't. It's not because I couldn't...well, all right."

And so, that night, Eeyore came to Kanga's house thinking he would just put Roo to bed, eat some thistles, and relax.

"Eeyore! Eeyore!" called Roo once Kanga had gone. "Come see my lovely new game." Out in the garden, Roo was turning somersaults over and over. "Try it. You're sure to like it!"

And although Eeyore tried his hardest to tell Roo differently, Roo was too busy chasing his tail to hear what Eeyore was saying.

So Eeyore said, "I'll just stand here and turn circles in a westerly direction, since eeyores don't flip over." And he did that until he was dizzy.

"That's wonderful, Eeyore," cried Roo, all excited. "Now let's run around the garden and then jump over the hedge!"

Eeyore was too dizzy to run and jump. "Not that you'd want to, Roo," he said, "but I think you should go to bed now."

"I will," said Roo, "just as soon as we hop up and down the stairs ten times!" Then Roo raced into the house and began to hop the stairs, and Eeyore could do nothing but follow.

"Roo," wheezed Eeyore, "sh…sh…shouldn't little roos be as…as…asleep?"

"No, roos should hop," answered Roo quite sweetly. "That's why I'm practicing now."

"Is that what roos do?" asked Eeyore gloomily. He was afraid Kanga would not think him very caring if he didn't get Roo to sleep on time. But then a brainy-type thought entered his head. He asked, "But tell me, where is it that a roo sleeps?"

"In his mother's pouch," replied Roo, "because it's soft, and warm, and cuddly."

"Then I know a game you must teach me."

"What is it?" cried Roo.

"I'd like to learn to be a kanga, but first I think I'll need a pouch."

And so Eeyore found a blanket and, following Roo's directions, folded it into a warm, cuddly pouch. Then, putting it around his neck, Eeyore said to Roo, "Guess it's time to test it, which is something only roos can do." So Roo climbed in and curled up.

When Kanga returned, she found Eeyore snoring loudly as he slept. Around his neck, tucked in a pouch, was a small, sleeping Roo. "Ah," said Kanga to herself, "I knew Eeyore would be good at this."

Tigger's Bounce

One bright spring morning when the weather was clear and a slight breeze blew in the trees, a bear of very little brain had a very good idea. "Let's go for a picnic, Piglet," Pooh said.

And so the friends packed up a basket—honey cakes, honeycomb, and honey pots for Pooh, haycorns for Piglet—and started for the river. Along the way they met Rabbit, and naturally invited him along. But at the river's edge, their trip went all wombly. The spring rains had washed away the trail to the eating spot.

But Pooh, who was always happy and hummy whether he was going or coming, suggested they jump on a log he'd found in the river and ride it downstream.

"Why, Pooh!" cried Rabbit. "You've had an idea! Although I can't think why, since you think so little."

Pooh asked what idea he had had.

unny

53

"We'll take these logs and make a raft to get to the eating spot," said Rabbit. Pooh had to admit he had been rather clever for a bear of little brain. When the raft was lashed together with bits and bobs of things, the friends pushed off from the shore.

Just as they did, who should appear but a very bouncy Tigger. "Where are you going?" Tigger called out.

"Down the river to the eating spot to have a bit of picnic," replied Pooh.

"Oooh, I love picnics!" cried Tigger, bouncing higher.

"Then come with us," said Pooh.

"Not if he's going to bounce!" Rabbit whispered. But he didn't say it loud enough. Tigger bounced right onto the raft, sending it teetering and tottering, shuddering and shaking, and making everyone wet!

"Off! Off!" yelled Rabbit.

The friends agreed there was really nothing else to be done, for a tigger has to bounce the way

the sun has to shine.

A very sad Tigger, his bounce small and meek, asked sadly, "May I picnic anyway if I follow you?"

"Of c-c-course," yelled Piglet in his strongest voice as the raft sailed downstream. And so Tigger bounced along the shore, playing in puddles, until he heard, "Help! Help!"

The raft was stuck, perched among rocks, in the middle of the river. It wouldn't move. It wouldn't budge. No amount of rocking would set the friends free.

"I'm coming!" yelled Tigger. At the thought of this, Rabbit covered his eyes. But Pooh's and Piglet's eyes grew larger and larger as they watched Tigger on the shore.

He started to bounce, and he bounced and he bounced, each time going higher and higher. Finally, when he was bouncing as high as a tree, he bounced right over to them and hit the raft right on its edge, setting it free!

"Yay!" cried Pooh.

"You can be the captain!" said Piglet.

Rabbit uncovered his eyes. Once they were on the shore, safe and dry and fed, Rabbit said, "Thank you, Tigger. We're lucky that bouncing is what tiggers do best!"

Fair-Weather Friends

The sky was dark and wet and full of wind howling through the Hundred-Acre Wood in a great hurry. Safe and dry in his cozy house, Piglet peeked out the window at the falling rain.

"Oh, my," he said as a loud clap of thunder made him jump. "Oh, my, my, my!" Piglet didn't care for such noisy storms. And even worse, he was all by himself!

I suppose I wouldn't be alone if I went over to visit Pooh, he thought, taking his new umbrella in hand. But just then, his whole house was lit with a bright, white light as a bolt of lightning flashed outside. Piglet dove headfirst under his bed and squeezed his eyes shut.

"On the other hand," he said through chattering teeth, "perhaps it would be best if I spent the rest of the night right here! I'm too afraid to go out on such a stormy night."

And so there he stayed for a very long time, covering his eyes when the lightning came, and covering his ears when it was the thunder's turn. *I do wish they would just get it over with,* he thought when the lightning and thunder came together so fast that he didn't have enough hands to block them both out.

He listened carefully to hear if the storm might be going away at last, when he noticed a new sound. **THUMP! THUMP! THUMP!** It came from his front door.

"W-w-who's there?" Piglet asked in a small voice as he opened the door just a crack.

"It's me," Eeyore sighed. "Caught in the rain. As usual." The water dripped off his back onto Piglet's rug, but Piglet didn't mind.

"I'm so glad you stopped in," Piglet said, running to get a towel.

"Thank you, Piglet," Eeyore said. "But I must be going now. I just wondered if you had an umbrella. I wouldn't want to show up at Pooh's house all wet, you know."

Piglet mopped up the puddles at Eeyore's feet and nodded. "Of course not. That would never do," he said. "You may use my new umbrella."

"I'd ask you along," said Eeyore, "but with just one umbrella, we'd each get half-wet."

"That's all right, Eeyore," said Piglet as his friend left. "Very small animals don't like to go out in very big storms. Although I do wish Pooh were here," he added sadly.

As Piglet closed the door, he felt more alone than ever. "Maybe I will go over to Pooh's, after all," he decided bravely. But then he remembered that Eeyore had his umbrella.

"Oh, bother," he said, jumping as one noisy thunder cloud crashed into another. He curled up in bed and pulled his quilt snug around his ears.

Piglet wasn't in bed for very long when he heard **THUMP! THUMP! THUMP!** at his front door again. Piglet bit his lip nervously. "W-w-who is it?" he called. But the only reply was another **THUMP!** on the door.

Holding his quilt around him, Piglet tiptoed to the door and opened it a teeny-tiny crack.

BOUNCE! BOUNCE! BOUNCE!

"Hoo-hoo-hoo!" laughed Tigger, rolling Piglet on his back as he bounced rainwater all over the room.

"Hello, Piglet!" said Pooh.

Piglet looked outside to see Pooh, Eeyore, and Rabbit, all trying to stand under his very own umbrella. "The best part about a rainstorm," Pooh said, "is spending it with your friends!"

And as he helped his friends dry off, Piglet couldn't have agreed more!